T0195942

# GOD CAN USE MY VOICE

Delaney Holley

For my Nana, who used her voice for God
in the ordinary moments of life, which
made an extraordinary impact.
Love you always and forever.

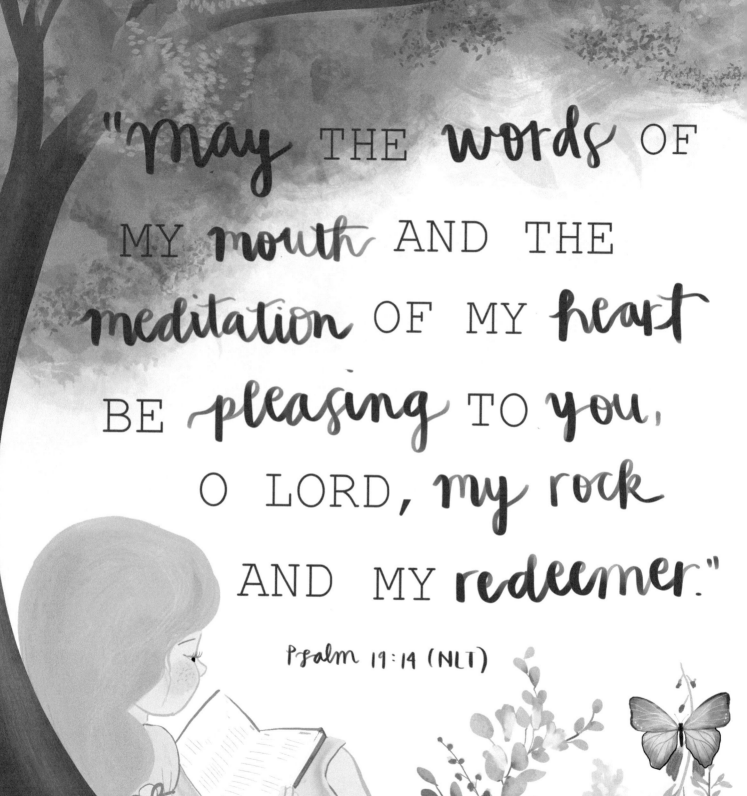

"May THE words OF MY mouth AND THE meditation OF MY heart BE pleasing TO you, O LORD, my rock AND MY redeemer."

Psalm 19:14 (NLT)

"That my heart may sing your praises and not be silent Lord my God, I will praise you forever"

Psalm 30:12 (NIV)

"Worry weighs a person down; an encouraging word cheers a person up"

Proverbs 12:25 (NLT)

As Willow skipped toward Honeycomb River to go fishing, she could hear God's creation singing their morning song. The bees were buzzing, the birds were chirping, and the flowers were dancing to the whistling of the warm breeze.

Willow smiled and thought, "Even the flowers are happy that it's Spring."

Willow was on her way to do one of her favorite springtime activities with her friends, Luke and Rosie.

HONEYCOMB RIVER

As Willow walked up to the river,
she waved at Luke and Rosie and said, "Good morning!"

"Look what I caught!"
Luke shouted proudly while looking at the fish.

"Wow! What a catch Luke!" Willow cheered.

"Hello!" Rosie sweetly told Willow.

Rosie was new to town and was so thankful to have friends like
Willow and Luke who were always so kind to her.

Willow asked, "Rosie, are you doing anything on Sunday?"

"No, I'm free as a kite!"

"Then you should come to church on Sunday with Luke and I!
We can sit together."

"Yes, come Rosie! You are going to love it," promised Luke.

"I have never been to church, so I would love to go!
I'll tell my parents!"

HONEYCOMB RIVER

As the sun filled Willow's room, she walked over to her window
to pray before church where Haven was waiting.

Haven would often join Willow in the mornings to hear her prayers.
Haven noticed that Willow sounded different in which she knew deep
in her heart that God loved her voice and that it was full of purpose!

Willow expressed to Haven, "I truly love the voice God gave me and I will proudly use it!" Haven smiled in approval while Willow began to pray.

Willow hummed happily as she walked up to the beautiful white church that she loved so much.

Rosie and Luke were already inside waiting for church to start.
As Willow walked up to her friends, she saw that Luke seemed sad,
so she asked, "What's wrong Luke?"

"I'm singing next Sunday at the church's Spring Recital. I'm very nervous about it. I feel like my voice is not good enough." Before Willow could respond, church began.

After church, Willow met her Nana in her garden.

"Hi Nana! Can I ask you something?"

"Hi honey! Of course, you can."

After Willow told her Nana about what Luke said at church, she asked "How can I help Luke?"

"Willow, you can use the voice God gave you to help your friend."

"In what way?"

"You can use your voice by praying for him and by speaking encouraging words to him."

"How will I know what to say, Nana?"

"Ask God and He will give you the words."

That night, while the crickets sang
and the stars twinkled, Willow used
her voice and prayed to God.

"Dear God, Thank you for my friend, Luke. He's very nervous right now about singing at church. I pray that Luke will feel your peace while singing. May he know how special his voice is to you, God. I pray that you will use his voice in a beautiful way. May he know that his voice is more than enough! Please give me the right words to say to Luke, that encourages him. Thank you, God, for my voice that you gave me. I love you.
In Jesus name,
Amen."

On a bright Sunday morning, Willow walked to church while praying and talking to Haven.

When Willow saw Luke,
she told him, "Luke your voice is more than enough and God
loves to hear it. Your voice is full of purpose and is special to
God. God can use your voice, Luke. Just sing to God when
you are up there and watch how God will use your voice as a
light to bless others."

"Amen! Thank you, Willow!"

As Luke walked towards the front of the church to perform for the Spring Recital, he remembered all that Willow had told him. He took a deep breath and began to sing to God.

Willow and Rosie ran to Luke after church telling him how amazing his performance was!

"Luke, thank you for using your voice today! I felt such joy while you were singing, which encouraged me to accept Jesus into my heart. So, I did!" Rosie gleamed.

"That makes me so happy, Rosie! Willow, you were right. God used my voice!"

With excitement, Willow ran to Honeycomb River to tell her Nana the good news! The news that God used her voice through an encouraging word and that God used Luke's voice through a song to bless Rosie.

"Willow, hearing this brings joy to my heart."

"God answered my prayers, Nana!"

"He always does and always will!"

HONEYCOMB RIVER

"Willow, keep using your voice for God. Promise me that
you will always let your words flow like how a river
flows. Let your voice carry the message God has placed
on your heart. Always remember this day, Willow, where
God used your voice."

"I promise, Nana."

# let the words flow

The voice you have given me, equipping me,
setting me free with the words you are telling me.

I run to you when I start to question.
Oh, in your presence, I touch the heavens.

When my words start to quiver, you show me the river.
Reminding me how a river flows, you invite the words to go, this is
when your glory shows.

The voice I try to silence, you say, is priceless.
Breathing possibilities that are ever so boundless.

How a river changes surroundings, your words have powerful abounding.

Calling me to speak, where you lead and make your ways complete.
This I know when I let the words flow.

When I respond with a "Yes" and start saying the words you spoke to my
heart.
You step in and do your part.

Now in a place of surrender, we can do this together.

I will not stand quiet, with you God, we will slay giants.

With my breath, you will bring strongholds to rest.

Words flowing.
Faith growing.
Your glory, showing.
Fear groaning.
Chains breaking.
Freedom overflowing.
This I know when I let the words flow.

# Kid's poem

When my words start to quiver,
you show me the river.
Reminding me how a river flows,
you invite the words to flow.
Calling me to speak,
where you lead
and make your ways complete.
When I respond with a "Yes" and start saying
the words you spoke to my heart.
You step in and do your part.
I will not stand quiet, with you God,
we will slay giants.
This I know
when I let the words flow.

# salvation prayer

Rosie used her voice to say a special prayer to accept Jesus into her heart and make Him her Lord and Savior. If you want to become a part of God's family and live a life with Jesus, you can use your voice to pray this prayer below!

Dear God, I come to you with joy in my heart. Thank you God, for sending your son Jesus, to die on the cross for me, so I can live forever with you! God, forgive me of my sins and help me live my life for you. Today I choose to receive you into my heart and make you my Lord and Savior. And from now on, I promise to do my best to live a life that is pleasing to you.
I love you, God, Amen.

You just made a wonderful decision by receiving and believing in Jesus! I'm praying for you as you follow Jesus and experience all that He has planned just for you!

And whatever you do, whether in word or deed, do it all in the name of the Lord Jesus, giving thanks to God the Father through Him."

Colossians 3:17 (NIV)

# letter from me

Dear friend,

I pray "God Can Use My Voice" was a blessing to you as much as it was a blessing to write. God has been speaking this message to my heart for years and I'm delighted that I get to share it with you. God transformed my heart to truly love the voice He gave me despite the deep insecurities of my stutter. After fully accepting the way God designed me, He then showed me the river. He whispered the words to my heart saying, "Delaney let your words flow, like how a river flows." God gave me this sweet visual to remind me to always let the message He has placed on my heart to flow freely with using the voice He has given me. Your voice is simply an instrument yet with God it can be turned into a beautiful melody for His glory. God can use your voice in the ordinary moments, in the unseen moments, or in the public moments of life but no matter where it is or what the message carries, God can use it to make an extraordinary impact. Your voice is wrapped with purpose and can graciously offer love, hope, and encouragement. A river has the ability to change an environment and with God, your voice has the ability to do the same! With God, your voice can help change the world for His glory. Willow and Luke used their voice to invite Rosie to church and that simple gesture led Rosie to accept Jesus into her heart. Willow used her voice by praying to God and speaking encouraging words to Luke that God gave her. Luke used his voice at church by singing to God. God can use your voice in endless ways just as He did for Willow and Luke. I'm praying that you will boldly and freely speak the words God has placed on your heart with the voice He has given you. So, my friend, what is God nudging you to say today? Use that voice of yours and let the words flow!
With wonder, watch how God will use it!

With love and prayer,
Delaney Holley

# meet us

**Delaney Holley,** author of *God Loves My Voice*, is an ordinary girl living for an extraordinary God. Delaney enjoys sunrises with the birds singing their morning song, anything crafty, handwritten notes, and loves teaching the word of God to the hearts of children. Delaney's heart is for God and her desire is to walk with the One who made her fearfully and wonderfully. Sharing the whispers spoken to her heart from God with words on paper and with the voice God has given her. Longing for others to fully embrace God's perfect design for them and to walk into their purpose with boldness and courage. Sharing how she struggled with disfluency in her life and how God transformed her to treasure her voice while trusting in His plan for her knowing that God loves her voice.

**Maria Jose Garcia,** illustrator of the book, was born and raised in Guatemala. Her passion for art started when she would make crafts with her grandmother, and eventually, her mother took her to art classes. Around ten years old, she found herself sketching floor plans of her dream art gallery. This inclination for building design would later guide her to discover her love for architecture as a career. As she grew up, God always continued guiding her steps. Throughout the years, she has been asked for several artwork commissions. Maria Jose paints a variety of mediums and styles. Art is part of her everyday life, and ultimately, she wants to use her talents for the glory of God.

WestBow Press books may be ordered through booksellers or by contacting:

WestBow Press
A Division of Thomas Nelson & Zondervan
1663 Liberty Drive
Bloomington, IN 47403
www.westbowpress.com
844-714-3454

ISBN: 978-1-6642-4626-3 (sc)
ISBN: 978-1-6642-4627-0 (e)

Library of Congress Control Number: 2021920333

Print information available on the last page.

WestBow Press rev. date: 10/11/2021

WESTBOW
PRESS®
A DIVISION OF THOMAS NELSON
& ZONDERVAN

Printed in the United States
by Baker & Taylor Publisher Services